GULITH

Mr. Biggs Goes To Town

Nelson S. Bond

Copyright © 2024 by GULITH NEW YORK IMPRINTS

ISBN: 978-1-63652-300-2

MR. BIGGS GOES TO TOWN

NELSON S. BOND

One thing is certain. When bigger and better shirts are made, the officials of the Corporation which underpays us will stuff 'em.

We were squatting in a cradle on Earth, waiting for flight orders, when the control turret door swung open and in marched two owl-eyed zombies dressed in frowns and white mess jackets. One of these looked at us, then at a slip of paper. He said, "Donovan, Herbert J.?"

"Present," I said, "but not accountable for. Otherwise known as 'Sparks.' What's the matter, Satyr? Who found out what about me?"

"Come," ordered the stranger curtly, "with me!" And he jerked a thumb in the general direction of the doorway.

Cap Hanson—he's the skipper of our space-shuttling freighter, the *Saturn*—bridled like a mick at an Orangeman's Ball. If there's one thing he cannot tolerate, it is hearing anyone else issue orders on his bridge. His brows congealed into fur-line cumulus clouds.

"And what," he demanded, "is the meaning of this, if I may ask, gentlemen?"

The other whiteclad studied him briefly.

"Hanson?" he queried. "Captain Waldemar V.?"

"That is my name, sir. And why—?"

"Come with me," said the second spectre, and diddled his digit like my accoster.

I said, "Not so fast, kiddies. Last time I followed a flickering phalange I ended up in an alley behind a Martian joy-joint with a headful of ache and a walletful of nothing. In words of one syllable, what's this all about?"

My answer came not from the pair before us, but from the entrance behind them. Through this came two figures. The foremost was that of my long-time friend and shipmate,

Lieutenant Lancelot Biggs; behind him was his uncle Prendergast, 1st Vice-president of the I.P.C. It was the older Biggs who spoke.

"It's all right, Sparks. These men are acting under company orders. They are medical officers assigned to give a physical examination to every man aboard the *Saturn*."

"Every man?" choked Cap Hanson. "Did you say *every* man, sir?"

I knew what he was thinking, and I felt a swift pang of compassion for the old boy. Hanson was one of the finest skippers who ever paced a quarterdeck. He had forgotten more space-lore than most men ever learn. But he wasn't as young as he used to be; not by about fifty odd years. Although Cap *looked* hale and hearty, his joints were beginning to stiffen like a mud-pie on Mercury, and sometimes, if you stood beside him in a quiet room, you could hear the dim clank and clatter of his arteries hardening. A physical examination might mean an end to his long career, exile from active service to the waffletail job he had long dreaded.

But old P. B. who, being an Earth-lubber, didn't know what grounding means to a true spaceman, just smiled.

"That's right, Captain. Every member of the command and crew is being examined. You see, the company is removing the *Saturn* from the freighter service—"

Removing! That was Jolt No. 2! Words got as far as my tonsils—and clogged there. But Biggs' uncle continued blandly:

"—and because of its magnificent service record on behalf of the Corporation, your ship is being assigned to new duties. Henceforth, the *Saturn* will lift gravs only on special tasks, assignments of vital importance which have proven too difficult for ordinary vessels of the fleet."

Well! That was something like! At last our efforts—or should I say the whackypot genius of Lancelot Biggs?—had earned us recognition. My weskit buttons tugged at their moorings; and glancing at my comrades, I saw they shared my pride. Cap Hanson's huge grin threatened to slice off the top of his head, while Lancelot Biggs' sensitive Adam's-apple was galloping up and down in his throat like a runaway yo-yo.

"Well, now!" said Hanson, gratified. "That bein' the case, I can quite understand why physical exams are necessary, sir. But do you feel that *everyone*—?"

"Everyone," nodded the Vice-president, "from highest to lowest. Everyone aboard this ship. Yes, Captain Hanson. Those orders have been issued, and cannot be altered."

Biggs gurgled happily, "Tell them what our first assignment is, Uncle Prenny."

"Ah, yes. Of course, Lancelot. Captain Hanson, you are doubtless cognizant of the—er—delicate situation upon the planetoid Iris?"

"Delicate!" I snorted. Of course Cap knew about it. We all did. It was the top-ranking scandal of the decade. A group of privateers, seeking a base from which to pursue their nefarious exploits, had established themselves upon innocent, helpless little Iris. There, though it was plain to everyone that the diminutive, rodent-like Irisians were being actually held in peonage, the corsairs had set up a puppet government, thereby procuring territorial rights against which the Interplanetary Council could not file demurrer. So:

"Delicate!" I snorted. "That situation smells worse than pole-pussy perfume in a telephone booth! What the Space Patrol ought to do is go in there and grab those rascals—"

"Sparks!" frowned the Old Man. "That will do!" But he turned questioning eyes to his superior. "Why *doesn't* the Space Patrol do something about it, sir?"

"Because," pointed out Uncle Prenny, "the privateers are—speaking from a purely legal standpoint—quite within their rights. The Patrol cannot move against them because to do so would be to violate the standards of freedom upon which the Interplanetary Union is founded."

"But everybody *knows* they're crooks ... pirates...."

"True. But by glancing back over the pages of man's history you will learn that it is always the crooks who twist law to serve their own evil purposes.

"These privateers moved to Iris, became citizens of that planetoid. Then, by brute force, they seized control of the political machine, voted themselves into governing power. With such power, it was an easy matter to pass laws forbidding exercise of Space Patrol rights of search and apprehension ... extradition ... prohibiting further immigration of peoples from civilized planets...."

I said, "Hey, wait a minute! There's one thing they *can't* do! According to interplanetary law, no government can forbid the right of free trade, barter and exchange!"

Lancelot's uncle smiled.

"Absolutely right, Sparks," he agreed. "And *that* is where *we* come in!"

A dead silence followed his pronouncement. Then the air began sizzling with a hot, frying sound. That was Hanson preparing to blow a verbal fuse. He exploded like a retread on a hot day.

"*So!*" he roared. "So that's the kind of a company I been workin' for all these years? Well, Vice-president, here's my rocket—" He tore his precious spaceman's emblem from his breast and hurled it to the floor—"and here's my brevet—" He ripped the golden epaulets from his coat, and heaved them after the rocket—"and the hell with you and the I.P.C., sir! Any outfit which would be so stinkin' niggardly as to *trade* with a crew of scoundrels like that—"

Lanse Biggs said mildly, "Now, Dad! Don't be hasty. After all—"

The Old Man stared at his First Mate and son-in-law sadly. "You, too, Lancelot? I'm disappointed in you, my boy. I never thought *you'd* fall in line with—"

Biggs' uncle said, "You are a very impetuous person, Captain Hanson. If you will let me continue—"

"I don't want to hear no more," growled Hanson. "Go 'way and leave me alone!"

"But let Uncle Prenny tell you, Dad!" pleaded Biggs.

"The hell with—"

"He can tell *me*," I broke in. "And if there's not a quick change of theme, I'm going to do a little snoot-poking before I leave—with the skipper. Go ahead, Mr. Biggs."

"You are *two* very impetuous men," decided Prendergast Biggs, "and I am surprised that you could think your employers would—but never mind. Let me assure you that we have no intention of dealing with these criminals on a friendly basis. On the contrary, we are going to do our utmost to break their grip on the suffering citizens of Iris.

"As Sparks has already commented, there is one thing the usurpers of Iris *cannot* legally do. That is, forbid the right of free trade and commerce between other planets and the captive Irisians.

"On the other hand, they *can* forbid the establishment of any community, outpost, or permanent trading-station upon their planetoid. They can prevent unwanted outsiders from becoming citizens of their base. In short, strangers may *visit* Iris, but they cannot stay there."

"Then, why—?" began the Old Man.

"However," continued the Vice-president, "there is a loophole they have overlooked. That is the clause in interplanetary law which reads: '*Any person or group of persons who discover, create or otherwise develop a hitherto undeveloped industry dependent upon the natural resources of any planet in the system are granted the privilege of establishing settlement upon that body for a period not to exceed thirty-five Solar years.*'"

He smiled at us. "That, gentlemen, is the entering-wedge with which we plan to crack the defenses of these tyrants who hold Iris in their grip!"

I stared at him confusedly.

"I don't get it, sir! You mean we're going into some kind of business on Iris?"

"Precisely, Sparks."

"But—but *what*? Iris is just a bleak little hunk of rock swinging in the Asteroid Belt. It doesn't have any soil to grow things in, any bodies of water to fish in. It doesn't *have* any 'natural resources' we can develop. So what excuse are we going to offer for barging into Iris?"

"We need no excuse for barging in, Sparks," pointed out Lancelot Biggs soberly. "It is our right and privilege to do so. All we need do is claim we mean to develop a new natural industry, and by space law they are forced to admit us for a ten day investigatory period. If by the end of that time we have proven our right to remain, they must let us do so. And we, being on Iris, can then call upon the

Space Patrol to 'protect' our property ... the Patrol can move in ... and wipe out the pirates."

"Sure!" snorted Cap Hanson. "Sure, that all sounds swell! But in ten measly days what new industry are we goin' to develop on Iris? Like Sparks says, they ain't no natural resources."

"Oh, that?" smiled Biggs' uncle Prendergast. "Why, that has already been arranged. We are going to make—*soap*!"

"S—soap!" gasped Cap Hanson.

"Soap!" I bleated. "Pardon me all to hell, sir, but somebody's crazy! Soap isn't a natural resource. It doesn't grow on trees or come up out of mines. You make it out of oil and fats and—"

"We're not thinking of that kind of soap, Sparks. I mean the form of hard soap used by miners, grease-monkeys and other manual laborers. Soap made out of pumice-stone. Our geological reports indicate that Iris, being composed mainly of igneous rock formations, is rich in pumice. All we have to do is locate an area rich in this material, start mining operations, and—bingo! We have Steichner and his crew of rascals right where we want them."

And that, lads and lassies, was Jolt No. 3! I knew about the Iris situation, but this was the first time I had ever heard the name of its kingpin and instigator. Hearing it, I winced. Steichner! Otto Steichner! The cunningest, meanest, toughest unhanged scoundrel who ever shoved a baby through an airlock—he was our antagonist!

I moaned feebly and pawed at my sagging jowls.

"Examine me quick, buddy," I begged the waiting doctor, "while my blood pressure is zero minus. Something tells me I don't *want* to go along on this expedition. Steichner!"

Lanse Biggs stared at me curiously.

"Why, don't tell me you're afraid, Sparks?"

"It's not that. It's just that I—I'm allergic to soap."

"Nonsense!" pooh-poohed his uncle. "Why, cleanliness is next to godliness, Donovan."

"That's what the rulebooks say," I conceded. "But in this case— cleanliness is next to insanity! Lead on, Sawbones. And here's hoping my veins are positively acrawl with something terrible...."

But no such luck! As it turned out, we didn't wait for the results of the medical examination to be tabulated before we lifted gravs. Something—I wouldn't know what—upset the routine, with the result that we took off that night for Iris. If you ask me, I think it was Cap Hanson's doings. I think he was afraid he might not pass the physical, and he wanted to be sure of being on the bridge for at least one more trip on the *Saturn*.

So we lifted gravs and with Lanse Biggs at the studs set course and traj for little Iris, a mere hop-skip-and-jump from Earth since we were using the V-I unit. For the first time in a long while, Diane Biggs didn't make the shuttle with us. Biggs' wife—the Old Man's daughter—wasn't feeling up to par. Neither was *I*, but they didn't give *me* any raincheck!

Anyhow, in just a little longer time than it takes to digest a day's victuals we were hovering in the strato a mile or so above the capital city of Iris, identifying ourselves to the port authorities on the ground below.

"Who are you," demanded the Iris dispatcher, "and what do you want here?"

"I.P.C. freighter *Saturn*," I tapped back, "requesting privilege to land under spacecode regulation 14, paragraph *iv*. May we come in?"

"Just a minute," advised my contact. He cleared and we waited breathlessly. When he came back again, it was on the telaudio rather than via the bug. The visor screen brightened, and we were looking into the scowling pan of none other than the big boss himself, Otto Steichner.

"Well?" he demanded.

Cap Hanson took over. He said boldly, "What seems to be the trouble, sir? We made a simple request for permission to land. We are an exploring expedition attempting to set up a new industry under spacecode regula—"

"I know all about that," growled Steichner. "Well, you're wasting your time, Captain. Iris has no natural resources, and wants no colonists. You'd better try somewhere else."

Cap said stolidly, "My Company's instructions—"

"Your Company be damned!" roared Steichner, his neck thickening darkly. "I control Iris, and I want no busybodies interfering with my—"

Biggs moved forward to the visor plate. When I say moved, I mean exactly that. Even his best friend could never honestly describe his peculiar means of locomotion as walking. His lanky frame lurches along in a cross between a gallop and a trot ... a sort of a bowlegged-pig-in-a-mirror-maze motion. He coughed embarrassedly, and his liquescent larynx performed incredible involutions.

He said, "Er—this is most distressing, Governor Steichner. Of course you realize that if we are not permitted to effect a landing we will be obliged to report the matter to our employers? And they, in turn, will naturally report it to the Space Patrol—"

Well, that did it. Steichner was playing a cautious, tricky game. Trying to get by within the barest shadow of the Law. In order to *bar* the Space Patrol from his domain, he had to live up to certain interplanetary regulations which forbade their marching in on him.

His eyes flashed dangerously, but he gave in.

"Very well, gentlemen. You may land. But remember! You have only ten days in which to prove there are natural resources upon Iris which you can develop commercially. If in that length of time you have not succeeded, you must leave."

"We understand that," said Biggs. "Thank you, sir!"

And so, unwanted guests of a most unwilling host, we laid the *Saturn* down in the lair of an acknowledged band of space-pirates. It was a piece of daring which, had I had time to consider it, would have given me more goose-pimples than a Siberian fan-dancer. But as it happened, I was too busy to bother about it. For, as Biggs was maneuvering the *Saturn* to its cradle, my bug started chattering, and it was Joe Marlowe calling from Lunar III. What he had to say was puh-lenty.

"That you, Donovan?" he tap-tapped. "Greetings, pal! They ache today?"

"What," I shot back, "are you talking about?"

"Your feet, of course. We just got the reports from the medical examiners. They say your tootsies are as flat as a pair of toed flounders. That makes you the same at both ends, doesn't it?"

I stiffened.

"Stop wasting juice," I advised him, "and give out. You got the reports? What do they say? Is the Old Man—"

"Sturdy," rattled Marlowe, "is the word for Hanson. Your Skipper's as chipper as a kipper. You're O.Q. Todd is O.Q. Bronson and McMurtrie and Anderson are O.Q. The crew checks one hundred percent. Enderby needs two teeth filled; otherwise O.Q.

Blaster Jacobs needs sun-lamp Vitamin C, but otherwise O.Q. As a matter of fact—"

One name was conspicuous by its absence. My gizzard turned over slowly. I interrupted, "Marlowe—look back over your list. Didn't you forget somebody? How about—?"

The answer came back slowly, almost sympathetically. Even over the dit-da-dits you can read expression in talented fingers. Marlowe tapped:

"I'm sorry, Donovan. I'm very sorry to have to tell you this, but there is one unfavorable report. The examiners have declared one man aboard the *Saturn* to be absolutely unfit for space travel. His heart is so bad that it may give out at any minute. That man is—First Officer Biggs!"

Well, there you are! Somehow I managed to take down the conclusion of the memo and sign off. But all the while I was doing so my brain was churning with the doleful tidings I had received; the thought kept repeating over and over again: "*Biggs—grounded! Lancelot Biggs—unfit for space travel!*"

My memory flashed back to the day when, almost three years ago, that tow-headed youngster had first gangled aboard the *Saturn*, fresh out of the Academy and not yet dry behind the ears. Fourth Mate he had been then, with no more responsibility than a laundress in a nudist camp. The Old Man had not liked him, partly because he was eccentric, mostly because he had avowed his intention of placing a gold band around the third finger, left hand, of the charmer whose name was at that time Diane Hanson.

But somehow Lanse Biggs had overcome these handicaps, by persistence worked himself up to the position of First Officer, by wit and guile and intelligence come through every obstacle set before him, by sheer determination proven to the skipper that he would make a good son-in-law.

His inventive genius had given mankind the velocity-intensifier unit, the uranium speech-trap, the first safe way of descending to the planet Jupiter—oh, why go on? Biggs' discoveries are as prominent as the Adam's-apple in his neck, and that's plenty outstanding!

But now, his future assured, his erratic past behind him, Biggs was to be exiled from the space he loved. Biggs—grounded! Lancelot Biggs—unfit for space travel!

So coursed my gloomy thoughts as I sat there in the silence of my radio turret. I did not even notice the *Saturn* was easing into a cradle. My first intimation that we were on Iris came with the arrival of Cap Hanson. He came burbling into my cubby, happy as a bee in a honeysuckle vine.

"O.Q., Sparks—we done it! We're on Iris. Shoot a message to Earth that we—Hey! What's the matter? Sick?"

Without a word I handed him my transcript of the report. He scanned it swiftly.

"Ah, the medical report, eh? Glory be, Sparks, this is wonderful! I passed! Isn't that swell? And you passed ... and Todd ... and...."

Then he stopped as abruptly as I had. A cloud swept across his forehead leaving his eyes darkened and sombre. In a whisper he said, "Lancelot—!"

I said, "That's the end of the chapter, Skipper. For three years the *Saturn* has been the finest ship in the fleet. We've done more tough jobs and had more fun than any bunch of spacemen who ever lifted gravs under the same emblem. But it ends now. When Lanse Biggs leaves this ship, nothing will be the same ever again."

"His heart," faltered the Old Man. "Who would have believed

there was anything wrong with his heart? I know he's skinny, and all that, but he always seemed healthy enough—"

"Where is he now?"

"What? Oh—outside. He's trying to make a purchase of some real estate, Sparks. It don't matter much just *where* he buys, so long as he buys. The whole asteroid's honeycombed with pumice pockets, you see. All we got to do is buy up some land, start diggin', produce hard soap and earn the right to remain here. But—his heart! Sparks, I can't believe—"

"Hush!" I warned him. "If those sounds aren't a herd of antelopes on rollerskates, I think that's him coming now."

Cap Hanson crumpled the flimsy, jammed it deep into his pocket.

"Not a word about this, Sparks! Not yet. We—we've got to break it gently!"

I nodded just as Biggs, grinning from ear to ear and back again, lurched into the turret. On his right arm he was carrying a queer looking little squeegee. At first I thought it was a teddy bear. Then it moved, and I realized I was in the presence of a native Irisian. He—or it—was a curious little squirrel-like creature with big, goggling eyes, a huge bushy tail and enormous whiskers.

Biggs chirruped cheerfully, "Here's one of the local boys, folks! Sparks, you speak Irisian, don't you? Well—"

He paused, glancing at each of us questioningly. "What's the matter? You two look as if you'd lost your best friend."

Cap Hanson essayed a laugh. It sounded like an echo from a torture chamber.

"Nothin' at all, son. We was just discussin' the difficulties of the problem ahead of us, that's all. So that's an Irisian, huh? And you can talk to it, Sparks?"

He looked at me with new respect. I smiled. "If my Academy prof wasn't just fooling," I told him, "I can." And I turned to the little rodent, twisting my lips into a series of purring whistles which meant "Greetings!"

"Phwee-twurdle-twurdle-pwwht!" replied the Irisian.

Cap Hanson looked at the asterite disconsolately.

"Needs oilin, don't he, Sparks?"

"Not a bit. That's his native tongue. He said how do you do."

"Yeah? Well, it didn't sound like it to me—"

Biggs suggested, "Ask him, Sparks. Ask him where we can buy or lease some property on Iris."

So I did. And the answer was encouraging. It seemed the little feller himself *chwee-fweeple-twee*—meaning he owned some property a few miles outside the capital city—and he'd be glad to sell us this patch of ground for *chirp-furdle-foo*—

I translated. Cap Hanson turned crimson with rage.

"Four thousand Earth credits! For a hunk of ground you could cover with a handkerchief? Ridiculous! We won't pay any such price—"

"It's no skin off our nose, Skipper," I reminded him. "The Corporation's paying for it."

Hanson nodded slowly.

"We-e-ell, maybe you got something there. We can't do no diggin' for soap without something to dig in. O.Q. Go ahead and make the deal, Sparks."

"And I," chimed in Biggs, "will organize the men and get to work on the digging—"

"No!" said Hanson hastily. "You mustn't exert yourself like that, boy. Remember your—"

He stopped abruptly. Lancelot glanced at him.

"What? Remember my *what*, Dad?"

"Nothin'. You stay here and direct the men; I'll get 'em onto the job."

So we became possessors of a bit of Iris terrain and set forth on the adventure which—we hoped—was to bring an end to Otto Steichner's rule over the tiny planetoid.

Of course you know that Iris is only a little hunk of cosmic debris, about three hundred miles in diameter, busting along in the planetoid Belt, just one of myriad specks which are all that remain of what was once upon a time a planet like Earth in the space-sector between Mars and Jupiter. It has no atmosphere of its own, so when you leave the domed cities and villages you have to wear your bulger, and since its gravitational attraction is about as strong as a two-day old kitten, you have to wear clinch-plates in your sandals.

But our boys are a tough crew, accustomed to working under even worse conditions than these, and I'm not bragging too much when I say that in two shakes of a rocket's tail we had staked out our property and buckled down to our task.

Our "task" was, of course, just plain digging. From that grayish-looking topsoil we had to peel away the crumbling layers which would lead us to the basaltic depths beneath. From this substratum we must extract a quantity of the pumice which was to justify our presence here. A simple thing.

Only it didn't turn out that way. It took us three days to scrape off the detritus layer. Then we reached rock. But it wasn't exactly the sort of rock we had expected to find: obsidian or basalt, lava flow. It was sandstone. Gray shale.

Lancelot Biggs looked at samples of this rock and shook his head. He said, "Hmmm! That's funny! Sandstone is not an igneous formation. You know—"

"I don't know nothin'," said the Old Man, "except we ain't got too much time to spare. Let's get on with our job."

So we kept on digging. We had to use atomotors. The rock layer was tougher than a blue-plate steak, but slowly our blaster chunked its way through ... to a layer of slate!

Cap Hanson said worriedly, "You reckon they might of made a mistake back on Earth, Lanse, boy? This here roofing material don't look like what we was supposed to find. Maybe there's pumice underneath, but—"

"Frankly," I said, "I doubt it. Pumice is the result of air bubbles mixing with an uncooled lava mixture. Slate is a sedimentary deposit. I think we've stumbled across a punk piece of ground, myself. We'd better go buy another hunk of property. Eh, Biggs?"

Lancelot Biggs said soberly, "If we want to locate pumice, I'm afraid so. I've been reading up on geological structure, and all the evidence indicates that—"

"Go see what you can do, then, Sparks," ordered the Old Man. "You're the only one of us which can talk Irisian. See if you can buy a nice soap-mine somewhere."

So I went. And I got nowhere—fast. The Irisian from whom we had bought this piece of property was nowhere to be found. He had "disappeared." No other native of the tiny planet would even listen to my pleas. The moment I started talking shop, they covered their fuzzy ears with furry claws and scuttled away.

Things began to make sense. In this maze of mystery I detected the fine touch of Otto Steichner. So I sought him in the armed citadel he called his gubernatorial White House. I put the question to him bluntly ... which does not necessarily mean "boldly," because to tell the truth my knees were shaking like a bowl of unchilled jello when I marched into his guarded study.

"Land?" repeated Steichner, "Land, Mr. Donovan? I'm afraid there is no property for sale on Iris. You see, everything here is owned by the government. Private individuals cannot buy or sell land."

I said, "But only five days ago we bought a piece of property from an Irisian named Tswrrrl. At the time, he mentioned that he had other properties for sale. But now I cannot seem to find him—"

"Tswrrl? Tswrrl? Ah, yes—" said the governor thoughtfully—"Tswrrrl! I remember now. An unfortunate incident. So careless of Tswrrrl. He was killed in an—er—accident a few days ago. Just the day before the Irisian government passed the new law forbidding the further sale of private properties, you know—"

"In other words," I said, "your bunch of thugs did him in? Is that it, Steichner?"

Steichner said silkily, "You do us an injustice, Mr. Donovan. We who control the government of Iris operate *within* the law at all times. That is why we find no need of allowing the Space Patrol within our sphere. Now, if you will excuse me? I am very busy—"

"In short," I said, "you don't intend to let us buy any more land. Is that it?"

"In short," replied Steichner, dropping his pretenses for a moment and giving me a stare which would have curdled a bottle of cream, "no! You have been given every legal opportunity, Mr.

Donovan. You have been here on Iris exactly five and one half Solar Constant days. If, within ten days after your arrival, you have not demonstrated your ability to produce a commercial commodity heretofore undeveloped on this planet, you will be asked to leave."

I rose. "O.Q., Steichner," I told him grimly. "You hold the chips, now. But let me tell you this—if we *do* find what we're looking for, and gain the right to remain on Iris, our *first move* will be to call in the Space Patrol to protect our property. And you know what that means. It means the end of you and your gang ... the end of your use of Iris as a base for marauding expeditions.

"You know that, Steichner. That's why you're—"

Steichner's face mottled unhealthily. He said in a gray voice, "You are talking dangerously, Donovan. Be careful no 'accident' stops *your* wagging tongue."

"If anything happens to me," I promised him, "you'll receive a visit from the Space Patrol before you can stutter 'nebular hypothesis,' Steichner. That's been arranged."

His lips were a white slit through which he gritted, "I quite understand, Donovan. But don't underestimate Otto Steichner. Even for *that* eventuality I am prepared. Now—get out!"

"Moreover—" I began.

"I said—*get out!*"

"So," I concluded my story to the skipper and Lanse Biggs, "I scrammed across the bridge and over the lake and up to camp, here. And thus endeth my little attempt to buy more land. It just can't be done, boys and girls. That's a dead duck."

The Old Man frowned. He said, "Yeah, there's no use squawkin' about it; Steichner holds the whip hand. The worst of it is, he'll probably be able to kick us off Iris without doin' a thing to bring in the Patrol. I mean, we'll get the gate strictly legal. Because we still ain't found no sign of pumice, and we're pretty deep now—Well, Lancelot?"

Biggs had been thinking. You can always tell when he's thinking, because his feet shuttle from side to side like spectators' heads at a tennis-match. Now he said, "Across the *what* and over the *what*, Sparks?"

"Seriatim," I told him, "bridge and lake. So what's that got to do with the present situation? The problem before the board is—"

"I was just wondering," commented Biggs, "how there should be a *lake* on the planetoid Iris—and why? As we know, there are no natural bodies of water on this tiny orb. Therefore they must be artificial—"

"All right," growled the skipper, "so they're phoney! Maybe Steichner's got a sense of beauty!"

"Sure," I agreed. "What he likes best is a lovely dagger, attractively decorated with nice, fresh blood. Cap's right, Biggs. We're not here to marvel at the scenic wonders of Iris. We've got a job to do, and we're getting nowhere—fast!"

"You mean," said Biggs, "our excavations? I've been thinking about that, too. And it is beginning to make sense to me. You know my motto, Sparks: 'Get the theory first!' I think I've solved the theory, now. The only thing which still remains is to put it into practice. But that lake—"

"You've solved it, Lanse, son?" broke in the Old Man eagerly. "Fine! Fine! I knew you wouldn't let us down. So what do we do?"

"Well, we must ask McMurtrie to rig up a hydraulic drill, first of all. Then we must—"

"Drill! To dig pumice? Son, you must be—"

Biggs shuffled embarrassedly.

"Well, it was only an idea, sir. Of course if you'd rather we can delve into the matter of that lake—"

"Never mind," said the Old Man hastily. "The drill it is. Anything to get your mind off that damn lagoon, O.Q. Issue the orders, Sparks."

So that was how we started boring instead of digging into the soil of Iris. And of course the shift of operations consumed still more of our ever-dwindling allotment of time. It took McMurtrie and his black gang a full day to rig up the hydraulic drill, and another day to set the cast so it would ram true. The next day we spent watching the diamondhead romp up and down in its casing, interrupting the steady *chug-chug!* every once in a while so Lancelot Biggs, who was watching the operation with the care and feverish attention of a mamma duck, could study the bore-facing.

He wiped his hand around the friction-heated facing and studied the granules. I craned over his shoulder and got a glimpse. I moaned.

"No go, Lanse. That *still* isn't pumice. I'm afraid Steichner wins. We've only got a little over one day to go, and it's no soap—hard *or* soft!"

But there was no discouragement in the eyes of Biggs. Instead, he was muttering with a sort of satisfaction, "Just as I thought. First shale ... then slate ... then this diatomaceous conglomerate. It is phenomenal, but it must be so. Sparks—" He turned to me suddenly—"Call Earth! Tell the authorities to dispatch fighting units of the Space Patrol immediately—to protect our property!"

"Our—?"

"Hurry! There's no time to waste. And—warn them to be very

careful in approaching this planetoid. They must make no attempt to land until we signal them the way is clear. Understand?"

"Of—of course," I stammered. "You mean you think Steichner will pit up a scrap rather than let them in. But are you sure you know what you're doing, Lanse? After all, a handful of grit—"

Biggs laughed triumphantly.

"But what grit, Sparks! What grit! See those bits of whitish colored substance?"

I looked again more closely at the powdery substance in the palm of his hand. I said, "Rock-measles?"

"Fossils, Sparks!"

"Fossils? But what have fossils got to do with—?"

"I can't tell you now. There is too much to be done, I've got to go down, for one thing, and have a look at that artificial lake beside the governor's mansion."

Cap Hanson, who had been off supervising the boring operations came up behind him just in time to overhear these final words. He asked.

"Still talkin' about that lake, Lancelot? What for? Why do you have to go down there and snoop around?"

"Because," explained Biggs, "I've been worrying about it, and I've just decided why it was built."

"Well?"

Biggs said slowly, "Steichner is a pirate; right?"

"Doubled and redoubled," I conceded, "in spades. So what?"

"We know he has a fleet of swift space-cruisers, no?"

"Yes."

"Well, then—*where are those cruisers?*"

I gulped and stared at him. So did Hanson. Then the two of us shook our heads and said together, "I don't know."

"Neither do I," admitted Biggs grimly, "for certain. But logic tells me it can be only one place. Hidden from view beneath the waters of that artificial lake—concealed, poised for deadly striking upon any unwary attacker!"

And there's an example of typical Biggsian reasoning. It had never occurred to either of us to wonder at the absence of a spacefleet we should have known must be somewhere around. But the moment Biggs hurled his bombshell we knew he must be right. It was the only explanation which satisfied the mystery of the lake on lakeless Iris. Steichner moored his spacecraft under water to hide them from the view of potentially hostile visitors. From their aqueous vantage-point they could emerge in the split of a second, guns spewing lethal flames to smash down the Patrol if and when the Patrol ever moved to capture Steichner's stronghold!

I yelped, "Great swooning serpents, let me get to my bug—" and started for the ship's radio. But Biggs grabbed my shoulder.

"Not so fast, Sparks! Don't send any warning about the lake in your message—not even in Company code. Steichner is a clever man. His experts might discover we knew their secret, and that would be just too bad—for us. We'd upset their applecart, yes; but we wouldn't be alive to enjoy the fruits of our victory. And—" He grinned wryly—"oddly enough, I have an ardent desire to keep on living."

It was the suddenness of his words which trapped the Old Man. He nodded and said reassuringly, "Of course, my boy. And you will. Why, these days a bum ticker doesn't mean anything. Lots of men have 'em and perk right along—"

Then he stopped, crimsoning, as he realized what he had said.

Biggs stared at him open-mouthed, then turned to me. I avoided his eyes. I couldn't help it. Biggs said, "Bum ticker, Dad?"

Hanson said miserably, "I'm sorry, boy. I meant to break it gentler than that, but it sort of slipped out."

"You mean—" said Biggs dazedly—"I didn't pass the physical examination? It—it showed my heart was bad?"

I nodded. "That's right, Lanse."

"But—but it can't be! I feel perfect. I—" His eyes darkened with a new fear. "I'll be grounded!" he cried.

Hanson said, "I'm sorry, son. But you'll still work for the Corporation, of course. And you'll have lots of time at home with Diane. It—it's even better than battin' around in space—"

But he wasn't kidding a soul. Least of all Lancelot Biggs who, for a moment, turned his back to us. When he again faced us there was a curious moisture in his eyes. Which, considering the fact that in the rarified atmosphere of Iris we were all wearing lightweight bulgers, could not have come from blowing dust.

He said in a low voice, "Well—get that message off, Sparks. I'll run on along about my errand. For if I'm not very much mistaken, we'll have visitors within the next few hours. As soon as Steichner's radiomen break down your code."

And he disappeared toward the city, a lean and lanky, somehow strangely forlorn looking Biggs....

Well, I sent the message. It cleared through Johnny Holmes at Long Island Spaceport, and Holmes was so excited he almost busted a finger on the key as he chattered back at me.

"No fooling, Donovan? You've succeeded in locating pumice?"

"We've succeeded in locating," I told him, "something. Don't ask me what. I'm only the hired help around here. But Biggs says it's O.Q., and whatever he says is all right with me. So goose the Rocketeers and get 'em on their way here as soon as possible—if not sooner."

"Right!" snapped Holmes. "Consider them started!"

So that was that. I wandered back to the digs, there waited for the second part of Biggs' prophecy to be fulfilled. It didn't take long. About four hours later—Earth standard, of course; you can't figure hours on a tiny planetoid which has no axial revolution—a monocar came blistering from the capital city to our encampment. It was packed to the gunwales, mostly with armed guards and Steichner. Steichner was packed to the gunwales, too, mostly with fury. He hurled himself from the speedster and strode to Hanson's side.

"Captain Hanson, may I ask the meaning of this?"

He jammed a sheet of paper under the Old Man's nose. On it was typed a complete, interpreted transcription of the message I had recently sent to Earth.

The skipper took it, studied it slowly, coolly. He said, "Same to you, Governor Steichner. May I ask how you got a copy of a message which was sent in private code?"

"That," blustered the politico, "is neither here nor there. My men are experts at deciphering such messages. What I demand to know is, by what right have you summoned a force of Space Patrolmen to *my* planet?"

The Old Man didn't know. He was as much in the dark as a blindfolded mole in a blackout. But he bluffed it through.

"Why," he said calmly, "under Regulation 19, section *xvii* of the spacecode, of course. To protect our property."

"Property?" roared Steichner. "*What* property? Don't try to pretend to me, sir, that you have succeeded in finding pumice on this terrain!"

I broke in, "So you even knew what we were searching for, eh, Steichner?"

"Naturally. I leave nothing to chance, gentlemen—nothing. Before your ship left Earth, I had been advised as to the trick by means of which you intended to gain a foothold on this asteroid. And care was taken that the property you were allowed to 'purchase'—at a handsome price, for which I thank you, gentlemen!—held no basaltic deposits.

"Well, Captain—answer me! Have you, or have you not, unearthed any pumice deposits?"

The answer came from a few rods away. Biggs had returned from his exploring trip. Now he took over, a fact for which the skipper was obviously grateful.

"The answer, Governor Steichner, is—no. We have not!"

"Ah! Then by what right, Lieutenant, did you summon the Patrol to Iris? You realize you were given but ten days to locate and develop a heretofore undeveloped industry upon Iris? And by your own admission, you have failed to find that for which you came—"

"True," admitted Biggs easily. "Quite true, Steichner. But though we have failed to find pumice, we have found something else. Another commodity never before exploited on Iris. We thereby earn the right to stay here for thirty-five years ... and to call in the Patrol to protect our rights...."

Steichner's fingers worked convulsively.

"*Another* product, sir? Out of this bleak, worthless soil! Impossible!"

And Biggs shook his head.

"Incredible, sir. But not impossible. Because, you see, it exists. Unless my latest estimates are completely in error, our drill should strike, at any minute now, a pocket of that substance which was created when Iris was still a part of a mighty planet swinging in an orbit between Mars and Jupiter. A commodity of great value ... an essential fuel...."

"What?" roared Steichner. "What are you talking about, you blithering idiot?"

Biggs didn't answer him. He didn't have to. For at that moment there rose a sudden warning shout from where our workers tended the diamondhead drill. Voices raised in swift alarm, from the ground beneath our feet came a strange roaring, rushing, gushing sound. And even as the workmen fled, the superstructure of our drill shattered and flew high into the thin air of Iris—borne aloft on a pillar of thick black goo!

There was an awful rushing sound and a column of black muck shot skyward.

And "*Oil!*" cried Lancelot Biggs triumphantly. "*Oil*, Steichner! That is the new industry which grants us the right to remain here!"

Well, it was a victory, all right—but for a minute I thought it was going to be a victory with flowers. For Otto Steichner's mouth turned livid with rage as he realized he had lost his tight grip on the planetoid Iris; his hand leaped to his belt, and for the space of a held breath I felt certain he would ray us all down in our tracks.

It was the oil which saved us. Pluming skyward, its jet hit a half-mile ceiling. Then, because Iris is not *entirely* airless, and has a *slight* gravitation, the column unbrellaed and splashed earthward. A viscous rain began splattering all around and over us. A greasy black torrent which turned us all into tar-babies before we could duck for shelter.

Steichner gasped, choked, and raced toward his monocar. But as his cohorts piled into it with him, he roared back at us:

"This isn't goodbye, gentlemen! I have other and more important things to take care of right now. But when I have disposed of the Space Patrol fleet, then I will return to take care of *you*!"

Out of range of the oily deluge, Cap Hanson turned a serious face to Biggs.

"Disposed of the Space Patrol? What does he mean?"

Biggs replied soberly, "I'm afraid he means just what he said, sir. My guess about the lake was right. It *is* the hiding place of his fleet. Steichner will flee there now, man his ships, and lie in wait for the Patrol. When the fleet arrives—"

I said, "Well, then, golly—let's lift the *Saturn* out of here! Beat it out into space, and stop the Fleet—?"

But Biggs shook his head.

"No—I have a better plan than that. Oh, Chief—" He called to Chief Engineer McMurtrie who, dripping with fuel oil and pride, was hobbling back toward the ship for a change of clothing—"nice work on that drill. Tell the men to cap the well for the time being. Did you get those metal poles I asked you for?"

"Yes, sorrr!"

"Good! And the silver?"

"About three tons of it, sorrr!"

"Silver?" broke in Hanson. "Three tons of it? Why, you must be talkin' about that specie shipment in the A-deck bins. You can't touch that, Lancelot. It ain't ours to use. It belongs to—"

"It belongs to humanity," declared Biggs. "No price is too high to pay for the overthrow of Steichner's crew."

He glanced at his wrist chrono.

"What time did you wire the Patrol, Sparks?"

"Eleven-oh-three-ack-em."

"Hmmm! They should arrive in less than six hours. We must get to work. All right, Chief. You know where I want those materials. And don't forget the salt!"

"No, sorrr!"

"Salt!" moaned Hanson. "Migawd, what now? You ain't goin' to cook and *eat* Steichner?"

Lancelot Biggs smiled tightly.

"No, not entirely. All I'm going to cook is his goose."

What happened in those next few hours makes sense to me now, but it didn't while it was going on. I'll admit that without a tremor. But, then, few ordinary mortals do understand what L. Biggs is driving at until he pops up at the end of his endeavors with a Q. E. D. clenched in his molars.

All I knew was, that by the time our gang got from the camp down to the capital city, Steichner and his crowd had disappeared. The city was empty save for a few assorted thousand fuzzy Irisians scampering around, whimpering dolefully because they didn't know what was going on.

Otto and his mobile units had taken a run-out powder. But, as Biggs had hunched it, they hadn't gone far. Just into their space-ships which lay a few yards below the placid surface of the artificial lake beside the governor's mansion.

Under Biggs' directions, McMurtrie's men got going. Their

first move was to dump a holdful of ordinary tablesalt, residue of a cargo we had never completely discharged, into the lake. That was screwy enough, and drew a murmur from the Old Man. His murmur changed to a moan when they followed this move by dumping into the lake those bins of silver ore which Biggs had mentioned.

Then came the whackiest part of all. Biggs implanted one of the two metal uprights MCMurtrie had forged for him in the southernmost extremity of the lake. Then—with the help of a tractor crew, of course; the things were twenty feet long—he set its mate at the other end of the lake, connected wires from the posts to the hypatomic motors of our ship.

All this took time, naturally. A lot of time. Maybe too much time. Because he had scarcely finished these preparations when there came a message from the commandant of the S.P. flagship:

"Ahoy, Iris! S.P. Cruiser Pollux approaching. Clear cradles for official landing!"

Our physical labor completed, we were back in my radio turret now. As we picked up this omniwave call, Biggs spun to me excitedly.

"Sparks—contact Steichner immediately!"

I twisted the dials, finally succeeded in picking up the wavelength of the submerged Irisian governor's set. Biggs spoke clearly over the audio.

"Governor Steichner, this is Lt. Lancelot Biggs aboard the *Saturn*. Can you hear me?"

Steichner's reply shot back savagely.

"I can, Lieutenant. Have patience. I will take care of you when this other little matter has been attended to."

"I called to warn you," said Biggs expressionlessly, "that you are in gravest peril. I am offering you a chance to surrender peaceably. Will you do so?"

Steichner's answer isn't printable. It was a blunt refusal. Biggs sighed.

"Very well, Governor. Then let me issue this final warning: Do not attempt to lift gravs from your present location! And do not attempt to use your ordnance. To do so will be to court instant and terrible death!"

"Why, you—!" spluttered back Steichner's retort.

But Biggs had turned from the audio, pressed a stud activating the hypoes of our ship. A dull growl surged about us as the powerful motors stirred into action.

I stared at him questioningly.

"What are you trying to do, Lanse? Scare Steichner into surrendering?"

"No, Sparks. I meant every word I said. Look at the lake."

I flashed on the visilens, swung it to cover outside. And what I saw there broke a gasp from my lips.

The surface of the lake was alive with tiny, frothy bubbles. The whole lake was seething with motion.

Cap Hanson cried, "Sweet saint, now I understand! You—you've turned that lake into a stew-kettle! You're boilin' 'em alive!"

"No!" I contradicted. "It can't be that. The ships are insulated against the absolute zero of space. Heat and cold mean nothing to them. Electricity! You must be electrocuting them, Biggs—?"

"You're *half* right," acknowledged my lanky friend. "Not electro*cuting*, though—"

He never finished his sentence. For at that moment there came to us over our still-connected audio the voice of Governor Otto Steichner issuing a command to his men.

"Fleet, prepare for action! Set studs! Battle formation! Set to lift gravs—"

"No!" cried Biggs. "Don't, Steichner! It will mean death to you all!"

"Ready!" rasped the stern voice. "Follow me! *Lift!*"

There sounded the rising tumult of mighty motors thundering into action. Then:

"The fools!" cried Lancelot Biggs pityingly. "The poor doomed fools! Why wouldn't they believe me?"

And my eyes swiveled to the visiplate once more, just in time to see the last act of the little drama. It came with terrible suddenness, devastating completeness. The waters of the churning lake boiled fiercely for a fraction of an instant as a half dozen spaceships jetted simultaneously. Then from the inwards of the lake, as from a gigantic steam-bomb, burst a violent sheet of flame. A coruscating, eye-blinding moment of brilliance ... then another ... and another ... six, all told.

Then—silence. Quietude. And the sad voice of Mr. Biggs saying, "Cut the connection, Chief McMurtrie. Our task is ended...."

I got it, then. I'm slow, but eventually I always straighten things out. I stared at Biggs with a sort of horrible fascination. I said, "So that's it. You didn't try to harm them. You simply *electro-plated their ships!*"

"That's it, Sparks," acknowledged Biggs sadly. "And when they attempted to jet from the lake, their blasts backfired against the silver barricade deposited over their ports. Their ships exploded like living bombs!"

Later, as our workmen reversed the polarity of Biggs' gigantic electroplating apparatus to reclaim as much as possible of the silver used in the operation, the commander of the Space Patrol fleet stopped by to offer his congratulations.

"It was a magnificent job, gentlemen," said he. "We commend you on having helped the System in ridding itself of one of its few remaining pestholes. Henceforth, the Irisians will govern themselves in freedom and contentment. Meanwhile, if your Corporation wishes to maintain its property rights on Iris, we shall of course honor your discovery of fuel oil."

He paused, staring at Biggs.

"But how did you know there was fuel oil on Iris, Mr. Biggs? Other geologists had never detected its presence."

Biggs flushed.

"I didn't know," he confessed. "As a matter of fact, I suspect that little oil-well will run itself dry in less than two days. You see, it can be but a tiny pocket, at most. The asteroid *is* mostly composed of igneous rock formations. My guess is that it comprised the side of a volcanic mountain on the planet of which it was once, ages ago, a part. When the planet exploded, a minute portion of the mountain valley was torn away with this fragment. It was from this ancient peat bog the oil derived.

"I began to guess there might be a vestige of oil when we dug up black slate. That is the invariable residue of submersion. Then, when we found the fossiliferous rocks, I knew we were on the right track. It—it was just luck."

"Well, luck or not," said the space officer heartily, "you certainly grasped every advantage which came your way. We need spacemen like you, Biggs!"

And—there it was again! For the first time in many hours, another reminder of the fate overhanging Biggs. Space needed men like Biggs ... but by virtue of a medical examination, he had been declared unfit for space travel!

The Old Man's face clouded. He said slowly, "There's another delicate problem. If Lance can't stand space travel, what are we goin' to do? Take him home, or leave him here on Iris?"

Biggs said resignedly, "You'd better call Earth and find out, Sparks."

So I contacted H.Q. And when I had asked my question there was a moment of silence. Then the bug-pounder on the other end of the connection said, "Do with Biggs? What do you *want* to do with him, Donovan? Why, bring him home, of course."

I said, "But if his heart won't stand the trip—"

"Heart? Heart? What's matter with Biggs' heart?"

"Why, the medico reported—"

"Oh, that!" pooh-poohed the Earth operator. "That was a mistake—didn't I tell you? The examiners got mixed up. It seems their orders were to examine *every* single man aboard the *Saturn*, with no exceptions. And since there were *two* Biggs on board—"

Biggs, who had been listening to the message come in, jerked like a spitballed schoolmarm.

"*Uncle Prenny!*" he yelled. "They got him mixed up with me. I'm the *First* Mate and he's the *First* Vice-president. They probably just entered the report that the 'First Officer' was unfit for space travel! Uncle Prenny's heart has been bad for thirty years!"

I grunted contentedly and cut the connection. "Then all's well," I said, "that ends swell, huh?"

The Old Man, too, grinned happily.

"Right you are, Sparks. From now on our troubles are over. Peace and contentment from now on...."

But with Biggs aboard the *Saturn*, that's a thousand-to-one shot. Any bets?

www.ingramcontent.com/pod-product-compliance
Lightning Source LLC
Chambersburg PA
CBHW071145250626
47159CB00006B/2304